O9-BUB-553

Dear Parent:

Your child's love of reading starts here!

Every child learns to read in a different way and at his or her own speed. Some go back and forth between reading levels and read favorite books again and again. Others read through each level in order. You can help your young reader improve and become more confident by encouraging his or her own interests and abilities. From books your child reads with you to the first books he or she reads alone, there are I Can Read Books for every stage of reading:

SHARED READING
Basic language, word repetition, and whimsical illustrations, ideal for sharing with your emergent reader

BEGINNING READING
Short sentences, familiar words, and simple concepts for children eager to read on their own

READING WITH HELP
Engaging stories, longer sentences, and language play for developing readers

READING ALONE
Complex plots, challenging vocabulary, and high-interest topics for the independent reader

I Can Read Books have introduced children to the joy of reading since 1957. Featuring award-winning authors and illustrators and a fabulous cast of beloved characters, I Can Read Books set the standard for beginning readers.

A lifetime of discovery begins with the magical words "I Can Read!"

Visit www.icanread.com for information on enriching your child's reading experience.

Fancy Nancy: Operation Fix Marabelle

ISBN 978-0-06-288871-6 (trade bdg.) — ISBN 978-0-06-284391-3 (pbk.)

20 21 22 23 24 LSCC   10 9 8 7 6 5 4 3 2 1
❖
First Edition

I Can Read!

Operation Fix Marabelle

Adapted by Nancy Parent
Based on the episode
by Laurie Israel

Illustrations by the
Disney Storybook
Art Team

HARPER
An Imprint of HarperCollinsPublishers

"*C'est fini!* All done!" I say.

 "Will Mr. Monkey be okay?"
asks my little sister, JoJo.

"*Oui,* yes," I tell her.

"I made Mr. Monkey all better."

"You are the best sister ever!"

says JoJo.

"Wow!" adds my best friend, Bree.

"That was amazing."

I am practically an expert
at fixing broken toys.
My secret to success is
I stay calm under pressure.

"See my hand shake?" I ask.

"No," says Bree.

"Exactly," I tell her.

As long as it doesn't shake,

I can fix any toy.

7

"You've got to do something
with this talent," says Bree.

"I can be a doll surgeon!" I say.

That's fancy for a doctor
who operates on patients.

Nurses Bree and Marabelle
will help me.
"We will fix the broken toys
and dolls of Oak Street!" I say.
Our doll hospital is open!

Lionel brings in our first patient.

It is his rubber chicken Bok Bok.

Bok Bok's legs are glued together.

Bree and I go to work.

"Cotton ball, soap, and water,"

I say to Nurse Bree.

Voilà! Now Bok Bok is all better.

Rhonda and Wanda arrive
carrying their lucky bobblehead.
"Our bobblehead stopped bobbling!"
they cry.
"Can you fix it?" asks Bree.

12

"I will take deep breaths," I say.

"I will stay calm."

I look at the bobblehead.

I see a marble stuck inside.

I pull it out.

"I'm next!" cries Grace.

She holds up her doll Penelope.

Her leg is twisted!

"Have you ever fixed a doll
this special?" asks Grace.
"Special dolls are my specialty,"
I assure her.

Grace cannot stay calm.
"Take deep breaths," I say.
"Think about the fun
you will have with Penelope
when she is better."

"We can go to Paris," Grace says.
"The real Paris, not the pretend one
in Nancy's backyard."
"There is too much noise.
Earmuffs, please," I say.

I fix Penelope's leg.

"Thank you," says Grace.

"I couldn't have done it

without my nurses," I say.

18

But when I reach for Marabelle,
I accidentally pull too hard.
"*Sacrebleu!* Oh no!" I cry.
Marabelle's arm has popped out
of its socket.

"You need to fix Marabelle!"
says Bree.

"Moi?" I say. "I'm too distressed!"

That's fancy for really upset.

"Then who will fix her?" asks Bree.

"You will," I tell her.

"We will help," volunteers Rhonda.

I go outside to the waiting room.

"You could tape her arm,"
says Lionel.
"You could tie her arm,"
says Rhonda.

22

Bree goes to work.

She pushes on Marabelle's arm.

Oh, no! It goes in too far.

She quickly pulls it out.

"We need Nancy Clancy,

doll surgeon," says Bree.

Bree comes outside to talk to me.

"I cannot fix Marabelle," she says.

"You have to do it, Nancy."

I start to shake.

"Take deep breaths," says Bree.

"Think happy thoughts.

Marabelle needs you."

I take a deep breath
and think about tea parties
and playing doll salon.
I am ready.
"Let's go fix Marabelle," I say.

26

My friends go outside to wait.

"Nurse, let's begin," I say to Bree.

"Powder puff, *s'il vous plait*!"

That's French for please.

I hold up Marabelle's arm.

Then Bree pours on glue.

We work slowly.

We work carefully.

C'est fini! All done.

Bree goes to tell our friends.

"You can see the patient now,"

she says.

"Great news," I tell them.

"The patient is *parfait*."

That's French for perfect.

30

Suddenly I am very tired.

I need a nap after operating.

"Why don't we let the doctor sleep,"

says Bree.

"Sweet dreams!"

Fancy Nancy's Fancy Words

These are the fancy words in this book:

C'est fini—French for all done

Oui—French for yes

Surgeon—a doctor who operates on patients

Voilà—French for look at that

Sacrebleu—French for oh no

Moi—French for me

Distressed—upset

S'il vous plait—French
  for please

Parfait—French for perfect